THE PIG IN THE DERBY HAT

Trussel and Gout: Paranormal Investigations No.1

M.A.Knights

White Harp Publishing

ISBN-13: 9798447870225
ISBN-10: 1477123456

Library of Congress Control Number: 2018675309
Printed in the United States of America

To Hayley,

Whithout whom Mr Gout could never be.

To
Victoria ,

Let in a Little

Magie !

Max

CONTENTS

PART ONE

I met Theophilius Gout for the very first time over a chocolate eclair filled with orange cream. The filling isn't strictly important, but Mr Gout, upon seeing this manuscript, made me promise to include it. After all, he said, life is all about those delectable little details.

He entered my parents' bakery at half past seven on a chilly November morning. The little bell above the entrance chimed, and I turned from stacking the loaves behind the counter to see him push open the door, advancing towards me with a solemn expression on his chubby face.

'My dear child. I am so very sorry.'

I regarded him in surprise, wiping my hands on my floury pinny. He was a large man, both tall and wide, with a somewhat roundish middle that tapered down to small, delicate feet. He moved with an unexpected lightness, bouncing on the balls of his feet, heels never quite touching the ground. A particular way of walking, as familiar to me now as the yellow-green tweed suit he wore.

'I do beg your pardon, sir. But whatever do you mean?'

He looked at me with his large blue eyes and shook his head. 'For one so young as yourself to face so much is just…just unthinkable!'

'Do I know you, sir?' I asked, sure that I did not. 'Are you in town for the hiring fair?'

'No,' he said. 'And yes. But of course, I refer to your baking.'

'I'm really very sorry, sir, but I'm not sure I understand you. Is there a problem with one of our products?'

'Quite the contrary, my dear, quite the contrary. Why, I'm sure I've never seen a finer display of patisserie in my life. Which is quite delightful for me, but for you, my poor girl…why, it must be frightful!'

'Must it?' I said, quite confused.

'It must! For the alchemy of baking is one of the most mysterious processes on Earth! The turning of simple flour, sugar, eggs and yeast into each and every delicious morsel in this shop…well, it is the very best magic I know. But for you…to have to go "behind the curtain", to have those mysteries explained in measures and weights.… Well, my heart breaks for you, it really does. I say, those eclairs look quite divine!'

He paid for his selection and I wrapped it in brown paper to take away. As he left, he forced an extra coin into my hand.

'So brave,' he said, fixing me with a beaming smile. 'Tell me, are your parents quite well?'

I blinked at the question. 'They're fine, thank you. Do you know them?'

'I see.' His smile slipped and an expression of deep thought appeared on his spherical face, before quickly being replaced with yet another smile. 'Oh no, not at all. Toodles!'

And with that he left, bouncing out into the lamplight and disappearing up the road. I stared after him for several moments. He had filled the shop entirely with his presence, and now it felt small and empty.

But soon other customers arrived, and I didn't think about the strange man again until I took lunch up to Granny.

'We had the oddest customer this morning,' I said as I sat myself down in the wicker chair at her bedside. Her small attic room was stuffy that morning and I longed to open the window, just a crack. But I knew better. Granny had always felt the cold, and during her bouts of 'infirmity' (my mother's word), she would complain that the merest breeze bit at her like Jack Frost himself.

Granny took a tentative sip of her broth. 'Odd in what way, dear?'

Broth was about all she could stomach when her illness came upon her. Even then she would eat precious little. On this occasion her infirmity had dragged on longer than usual, leaving her scarcely more than a pile of bones beneath her sheet and blanket. In truth, I worried about her. Her white hair, shiny and bouncy in health, lay flat and dry against her pillow. The pink highlights on her cheeks that shone out when she laughed or drank sherry had all but disappeared, her face almost as white as her hair.

I'd expressed my concern to Mother just the previous day, and she had frowned at me sadly.

'Granny is an old woman now,' she'd said, working the dough with both hands as she spoke. 'We must accept that she will not live forever. It is time for us to get used to the idea of life without her.'

I knew this, of course, but it was hard to see her so frail and shrunken when between episodes of illness she was as healthy as the best of us.

'Odd in manner,' I explained to her as she played with the broth. 'He seemed to have the most peculiar notions about baking.' I told her what he had said to me and Granny laughed; a wheezing, rattling sound.

'I'm sorry I missed him. He sounds like an interesting gentleman. Is he here for the hiring fair?'

'I think so.'

'Well, be careful your mother doesn't sell you to him for the price of a few bags of flour, then.' Granny's lips thinned as she spoke.

I didn't reply. My going off to work for a wealthy family was a source of some contention in our little family. My mother was pushing for it.

'We could really use the extra money, Clementine, dear,' she kept saying.

Granny, on the other hand, was dead against it.

'She needs to stay here and continue her training in the bakery!' she would snap whenever the subject was raised.

My father remained resolutely silent on the matter, knowing the women under his roof well enough to refrain from getting caught in the middle. I scarcely knew how I felt about it. All I could think about was who would care for Granny if I were to leave. Mother and Father were too busy, and my three younger brothers still too young to take the charge seriously.

Never-the-less that afternoon found me in Fairsop's market square as the hiring fair officially opened. You could barely see the cobbles for the crush of people, many wearing their Sunday finery, faces scrubbed pink in the weak afternoon sun. There were cowmen carrying their wisps of straw, shepherds holding their crooks aloft, dairymaids with their pails, and housemaids with their brooms and mops, each item denoting their chosen profession. All of them jostled for the most visible positions, shouting out their special skills and attempting to catch the eye of potential employers. A lucrative year for many families depended on deals struck that day, and competition was fierce.

Some in the crowd wore bright ribbons, accompanied by even brighter smiles, indicating they had already attracted employment. Booths selling pies, chestnuts and eels, or offering games, stood all around the square, tempting them to spend their fastening-penny; the name given to the shilling presented to each by their new employers, sealing the deal. The Golden Fleece, Fairsop's most popular inn, was already doing a fine trade and the sound of drunken revelry mingled with the hubbub of the fair, so people had to shout if they wanted to be heard above the din.

I stood in my best dress on the outskirts of the throng, awkwardly clutching my broom, a rolling pin tucked into the pocket of my freshly laundered apron. It was then, as I nervously watched the crowd, trying to pluck up the courage to attract a potential employer, that I saw Mr Gout for the second time. He bobbed in and out of the crush, a ball of yellow-green tweed, talking to the townspeople, patronising the food stalls, but never, did it seem, actually making any deals. I watched him with interest, fascinated by his strange mannerisms. He seemed almost another species to the villagers and other employers; a tweed-coated interloper. Eventually, he drifted in my direction and, on spotting me, came over with a beaming smile.

'Well, hello again, my dear girl!'

'Clementine,' I said. 'Clementine Trussel. I'm sorry, I didn't catch your name before.'

'Gout, my dear; Theophilius Gout. Are you looking for work?' He took in my broom with a curious eye.

'Oh, well...yes!' I said, a little awkwardly. 'I can clean, light fires, cook, and bake, of course.'

'I don't doubt it for a second, my dear,' he replied with a smile. 'But I'm a little surprised. I'd have thought the bakery would keep you busy enough.'

'The extra money would be useful. My grandmother is ill, you see, sir.'

This seemed to pique Mr Gout's interest and he looked at me with large, earnest eyes. 'I'm very sorry to hear it. Nothing too serious, I hope?'

I explained Granny's symptoms, her ups and downs, and how the illness seemed to be lingering on this occasion. Mr Gout listened with great interest and it was only after I finished I wondered why I had divulged so much to a complete stranger.

'Strange indeed,' he said, stroking his smooth, round chin.

There followed a beat or two of silence while Mr Gout stared off into the middle distance. I cleared my throat and said, 'Would you happen to be looking for a maid or housekeeper, sir? I'm a very hard worker.'

His eyes slid slowly back to mine, as though he had momentarily forgotten I was there. 'I already have a housekeeper,' he admitted.

'Oh,' I said, a little disappointed.

'But I am perhaps in the market for a housekeeper's assistant,' he continued. 'Mrs Winchester is not as young as she once was. I dare say she would welcome the help. And it would be nice to have a baker in the house!'

'Mrs Winchester doesn't bake?' I asked, hope blossoming.

Mr Gout gave a little grimace. 'She is a wonderful woman. Splendid. Radiant. An ambassador, a queen, an empress! But my dear, you should taste her Victoria sponge…dreadful! She suffers, I'm afraid to say, from that most unfortunate malady of the home baker: a soggy bottom. And yet she somehow manages to dry out the edges!'

'It can't be that bad, surely, Mr Gout?' I said, laughing.

'She uses tinned strawberries, my dear Clementine. Tinned! It does my delicate constitution no good at all.' He closed his eyes with a shudder.

'Well, perhaps we could come to some arrangement?' I suggested.

'Yes, perhaps we could! Well, good afternoon, Miss Trussel. Do keep a close eye on your grandmother, won't you?' And, with a touch of his hand to his forelock, he turned and walked away without another word. I gaped after him, baffled. Had I said something wrong?

The rest of the afternoon proved just as fruitless, and as the wintry sun faded, I turned for home with mixed feelings. Mother would be angry I had not found myself a position, but I couldn't help feel relieved I could remain to look after Granny. I planned to check on her as soon as I got home.

Mr Gout's last words to me echoed in my ears, and as the bakery came into sight, my eyes searched for her small attic window. The shadows in our street were already deepening, but I could still see well enough to catch a flash of moving glass and a dark form dropping from my grandmother's window, which was open. I stopped in surprise.

The next house along blocked my view, so I didn't

see the thing reach the ground. But I could have sworn I heard the faintest thud of it hitting the little dirt alley that ran between our premises and our neighbours. What had it been?

I suddenly felt very alone in the empty street. The alley was a dead end, meaning anything that had fallen into it would have to leave via the main street. I held my breath and watched the alley entrance, not daring to move any closer. Then, to my utter astonishment, a small pig exited the alley at a run, its little trotters skittering on the cobbles as it moved up the street away from me. As a market town, it was not unheard of for livestock to be found wandering the streets of Fairsop. But what so surprised me about this particular beast was the tiny black derby hat perched between its piggy ears. There was even a green feather stuck through the band. I watched, dumbstruck, as the pig trotted off into the distance, then turned the corner and disappeared.

'Well now, there's a thing and no mistake,' said a voice behind me, making me jump. I turned to see Mr Gout stood not twenty paces away.

'Did you see that pig?' I asked, unsure what else to say.

'I most certainly did, my dear Clementine, and I think we had better check on your grandmother right away.'

PART TWO

He was wearing an expression of deep concern, in such contrast to his usual cheer, that I agreed without further question. I led him into our house via the side door, as the shop was already locked and the blinds drawn closed. We entered our little sitting room, but there was no sign of my parents, who were probably cashing up the day's takings.

Wordlessly, I led the way up to Granny's room. All was dark and still within, the only sound Granny's laboured breathing. Mr Gout had to duck his head slightly to enter, and once inside his ample frame made the room seem even smaller than usual. I squeezed past him and fumbled with the paraffin lamp and box of matches on the bedside table until a soft yellow glow chased back some of the shadows. I looked down at my grandmother's sleeping form and gave a little cry. Her face was grey, cheeks hollow and her eyes like sunken pebbles beneath her closed lids, in sockets much too large. She might have been dead, but for her continued ragged breath. She looked so much worse than when I had seen her at lunch.

'Granny?' I whispered, not wanting to startle her. There was no response. 'Grandma!' I said, a little louder. Still nothing.

'I wonder if I might take a look at her?' Mr Gout asked, kindly but firmly ushering me to one side so that he could manoeuvre himself into a stooping position over the bed. He felt at Granny's wrist for a pulse, timing it on a pocket watch fished from his jacket. Next, with a surprisingly gentle touch, he peeled back her eyelids with his porky fingers, examining first one, then the other closely. Finally, he pulled back the covers, revealing the almost skeletal chest of my grandmother in her nightdress.

'What are you doing?' I was shocked, and suddenly wondering what on earth had possessed me to let this man into my home.

'Nothing untoward, I assure you. But there is something I must check.' He eased aside the neckline of my grandmother's nightdress to reveal an angry purple bruise that appeared to stretch right across her chest.

'What's that?' I gasped.

Mr Gout carefully straightened the neckline, then re-covered Granny with her blanket before stepping back and looking at me with serious eyes.

'Tell me, Clementine, have you ever noticed anyone coming or going from your grandmother's room before tonight?'

'No,' I said, a little startled by the question. 'Apart from myself and my parents, of course. My brothers hardly ever come up here.'

'And has your grandmother herself ever complained of nightly visitors?'

'Most certainly not! This is a respectable house, Mr Gout!'

'Of course, my dear. I would not dream of asserting otherwise.'

'What is going on? Will Granny live, do you think?'

'I fear that may well rest on our actions over the next twenty-four hours. She is very weak. I'm afraid she will not survive another attack.'

'Attack? What on earth do you mean, Mr Gout?'

'I think it best we leave your grandmother to rest and retreat to your charming sitting room. A nice calming cup of tea, perhaps?'

Once again, I found myself agreeing with this strange man, and I led him back down the stairs to our humble sitting room. I invited him to sit and there were an awkward few moments whilst he extracted himself from our leather tub chair; it proving too modest for his ample frame. He eventually seated himself on our more forgiving sofa and I went to make the tea. Once the water boiled, as an afterthought, I added two slices of Victoria sponge to the tray and re-joined my guest. Mr Gout clapped his podgy hands together in delight.

'Miss Trussel, you astound me with your generosity! And we were just talking about this very cake this afternoon.'

'It's nothing, sir.' I blushed slightly. 'I made it yesterday, and it needs eating.'

'Well then, I'm your man!' he said, taking one of the little plates I'd put out and sitting back with every sign of contentment. I watched him, suddenly uncomfortably aware that I was sitting alone with a male stranger; hardly a respectable thing for a girl of my age. But there was something about Mr Gout. The longer I spent in his presence, the more I found myself agreeing to whatever he suggested.

'You were talking about some kind of attack?' I prodded.

'Yes, dreadful business! Quite ghastly. I say, is this vanilla sugar sprinkled on top?'

'Er, yes.'

'Quite divine!'

'You were saying, Mr Gout?'

'Hmmm?'

'The dreadful business?'

'Oh yes, of course. Tell me, my dear Clementine, have you ever heard of such a thing as an Alp?'

I thought hard, but the word had little meaning to me then. 'I don't believe I have. Is that what you think attacked Granny? Is…is it a type of pig?' I felt stupid even as the words left my mouth.

Mr Gout gave a little chuckle. 'Aha, no. Although it can appear to look like one, as you yourself saw not an hour ago.'

'So that thing…the pig in the hat…that was an Alp?' I asked, trying to understand.

Mr Gout took another large mouthful of cake before responding out of the side of his mouth. 'I believe so, yes. An Alp, my dear, is not a type of pig but a shapeshifter that can appear as any number of things. It is a trapped, wandering soul, obliged to feed off its victims' life force to survive.'

I stared at him. I was not, at this point in my young life, much prone to thoughts about the supernatural. Fairsop was a quiet town. My life revolved around the bakery, looking after Granny, and the occasional day helping out one of the farmers during harvest time. I had never travelled further than three miles from the very spot where we sat on that dark November evening. But as my eyes were drawn to the small window, and the lamp-lit street beyond, I felt, with a certainty that I still cannot fully explain, that this peculiar gentleman sat opposite me was right.

'So...so those bruises?'

'Were caused by the Alp's weight on your grandmother's chest as it fed, yes.'

'That's horrible!'

Mr Gout nodded his head sagely whilst licking the remains of cake from his fingers. Then a thought occurred to me.

'So that would mean that these episodes of infirmity my Granny suffers...they've been caused by an Alp every time?'

'Almost certainly,' Mr Gout said. 'It is common, once the creature has chosen its victim, for it to revisit them many times, sometimes years between attacks.'

'That...would explain a lot.'

Mr Gout looked at me appraisingly. 'I must say, Miss Trussel, you're taking this very well. It takes some people a good deal longer to accept the facts in front of them.'

I returned his gaze. 'There is something about you, Mr Gout. I find myself trusting what you say. I'm guessing you have some experience with this sort of thing?'

'I have encountered one or two oddities in my life,' he admitted with a smile. 'And even helped to resolve some unfortunate events.'

'It's why you're here, isn't it? To stop the Alp?'

He grinned at me. 'Very good. To resolve the situation, yes.'

'Did...did you already know? This morning, in the bakery, when you asked about my parents?' I asked, more accusingly than I'd intended.

But the man shook his head firmly. 'I'd heard rumours, that's all. An old acquaintance of mine travelled through your charming town some weeks ago and saw something odd. He wrote to me about it, knowing my interest in such matters.'

'What did he see?'

'A dog, wearing a black derby hat, with a green feather. The hat, you see, is the source of much of an Alp's powers. A Tarnkappe, in the early German records. It is what allows the spirit to change its shape, although the Tarnkappe itself will always remain visible. So I have been searching the town for further clues. More sightings, unexplained illness, that sort of thing. Are you going to eat that?'

'Er...you go ahead,' I said, surprised by the sudden change in his tone. He reached for the second slice of cake with a greedy smile. 'So, do we need to destroy the hat? Will that stop the Alp?'

Mr Gout frowned at me over the slice of Victoria sponge. 'Technically. The Tarnkappe's destruction would mean the Alp could no longer take on any other than its true form. But I would rather avoid such drastic action.'

'What on earth for?' I said. 'This thing is trying to eat my grandmother!'

He lowered the cake back onto the plate and fixed me with his penetrating blue eyes. 'But remember, an Alp is a lost spirit, meaning it was once human. Separating it from the hat will not release it. I would much rather find a way to bring it peace. Only then will the spirit be free, and your grandmother as well.'

'Oh,' I said, a little abashed.

'Incidentally, did you mean what you said before?' Mr Gout asked after a few moments, picking up the slice of cake once more.

I hesitated, unsure what he meant.

'You asked if we needed to destroy the hat. Am I to assume you intend to become involved?' he prompted as the Victoria sponge disappeared into his open mouth.

I thought for a moment. 'It seems to me that I am already involved. And I will do whatever it takes to save Granny.'

'Excellent!' He smacked his lips appreciatively. 'In

which case, we should begin first thing in the morning. But before I leave you, I simply must have a spot of this tea you so lovingly prepared for us. I always find cake requires a little tea to follow, don't you?'

The next morning came pallid and misty. I left the house just after dawn, slipping out while my parents were busy in the bakehouse. Granny's condition had changed little overnight, and I was eager to help her. I had agreed to meet Mr Gout on the outskirts of town, by a lake known locally as the sheep dip. He hadn't explained why he wanted to meet there and I hadn't pressed him.

Our conversation the previous evening had left me with much to think about, and it seemed to me, if I was prepared to take his word on this Alp business, then I could trust that he had his reasons. Regardless, I had not slept well. I couldn't stop thinking about the Alp. That something so horrid had been in our house – possibly visiting regularly for years – unsettled me greatly. As I moved through the grey town I jumped at every movement, eyeing other early risers with mistrust. Familiar streets felt strange and threatening. So it was I arrived at the sheep dip with a deep sense of dread in my heart.

Fortunately, Mr Gout had arrived before me and was standing by the misty water's edge in a brown tweed ulster coat, its elbow-length cape stirring in the gentle breeze coming off the water. As I approached him, I saw he was holding what appeared to be an egg between one finger and thumb, examining it intently.

'Good morning, sir.'

'Do you suppose this is a duck's egg or a hen's egg?' he asked without looking at me.

'Um…it looks too small to be a duck's egg,' I ventured, marvelling again at the strange way the man deported himself.

'That's what I thought,' he agreed with a glum look. 'I asked for duck. I'll have to have a word with the landlord at The Golden Fleece. This is quite unacceptable!'

He rapped the egg hard against the knuckles of his other hand, then rolled it up and down his arm, cracking the shell before beginning to peel it.

'Are you staying at The Golden Fleece, sir?' I asked, unsure of what else to say.

He turned his face to me for the first time and smiled. 'Yes. Charming place. Very good beef. But where are my manners? Good morning, my dear girl!'

'Good morning,' I repeated.

'Have you breakfasted?'

'Not yet; we usually just grab something on the go, what with the bakery to open.'

Mr Gout looked aghast. 'But my dear Clementine, breakfast is quite simply the most important meal of the day! The Inn was good enough to serve me a morsel or two before I left this morning. Porridge, haddock, bacon, fried potatoes. Oh, and a very fine pair of kippers.' He counted each item off on his fingers with relish.

'Oh, I couldn't possibly eat all that so early,' I said. 'I'll be fine until later.'

Mr Gout looked unconvinced, and I watched his face fall as he appeared to realise something. He looked at his peeled egg with great regret, then thrust it towards me. 'Here. Your needs are greater than mine.'

'Oh, no, really Mr Gout, I'm quite alright.'

'Are you sure?' Hope re-entered his chubby features.

'Quite,' I insisted.

His hand withdrew sharply, and the egg was rapidly inserted whole into his mouth as if he were afraid I'd change my mind.

'Splendid!' he said around it, beaming at me once more. 'To business then! This lake is where my friend described seeing the dog in the hat. So I think there is a good chance the Alp has made its lair somewhere around the water's edge.'

'How do we find it?' I asked.

'By looking, dear girl. No shortcuts for this type of work, I'm afraid. That's why I had us meet so early. Alps rarely show themselves in full daylight, so we have a good few hours to search the lake before it stirs.'

'Then I suppose we should get started,' I said, looking at the gloomy vegetation at the water's edge. 'Is there anything particular to look out for?'

'A large hole, simply put,' Mr Gout said. 'A sort or burrow, big enough for a man to crawl inside, for an Alp will return to its original form when it sleeps.'

'So it will look human?'

Mr Gout made a face. 'Not exactly, no. It is technically dead, after all. How much of its original form it remembers will depend somewhat on how long it has been dead. It might make for a...disturbing sight.'

I nodded, suppressing the image that popped into my head. 'And if we find it? What do we do then?'

He winked and patted the pocket of his coat, which was bulging from something secreted inside. 'Leave that to me, my dear. Should we happen across the beast it would be best if you keep your distance and leave tackling it to my more experienced hands. Agreed?'

I nodded. 'Of course. I'll stay well back.'

We began our search, pushing through the wet undergrowth, scanning the ground in the pale light. It wasn't long before my skirts were soaked and my back was aching from the awkward stoop I was required to adopt. My initial enthusiasm shrank with every passing minute.

We worked our way steadily around the lake as the sun rose higher in the sky. By the time it was overhead, even Mr Gout's good humour was waning.

'I must admit, I rather hoped we'd have found it by now,' he grumbled, straightening up and stretching out his back with a grimace. 'But that's the supernatural for you; always popping up when you don't want it, then disappearing when you do!'

'Do you think we have the wrong place?' I asked, also trying to ease my protesting back.

My companion shook his head. 'No, I'm sure it's here somewhere, blast the damn thing!' He looked at me guiltily before adding, 'I'm so sorry, Miss Trussel; please excuse my language.'

In truth, I'd heard my father say worse on many occasions. I smiled. 'That's quite alright, Mr Gout. It's been a trying morning.'

'It has!' he agreed with a sigh. 'I should have packed a lunch. I wonder if there are still any blackberries about?' He poked a patch of brambles next to him with his foot, then rocked back in alarm, stumbling and falling onto his great behind as something large erupted out of the undergrowth in his face. The thing landed on all fours between us, growling and hissing like no animal I had ever seen. It was human-shaped, at least passably, with mottled blue-green skin that shone wet in the midday sun. It looked emaciated, its ribcage and other bones sticking out through its meagre flesh, whilst what remained of its hair fell in lank, tangled strings around its shoulders. Its face had a large emphasis on teeth and a thin, forked tongue flicked in and out of its mouth as if it were tasting the air. The black derby hat was on its head, a bizarre touch of civilisation that made the rest of the beast seem all the more monstrous.

I registered all this in one horrified second before the beast sprang up again and dashed away through the scrub, disappearing from view.

'Theophilius, you blundering buffoon!' Mr Gout cried, admonishing himself as he struggled to his feet. 'A fine show you've made of yourself! Are you unharmed, Miss Trussel?'

I nodded mutely.

'Well, that's something, at least,' he said bitterly.

'Was...was that the Alp?' I stammered.

'*Was* is the operative word,' Mr Gout replied. 'Because it's long gone now.' He rummaged around the area by his feet, revealing disturbed earth and the entrance to a burrow about two feet across. 'Yes, there it is. Fat lot of good it'll do us now. We may as well head back to town and regroup, Miss Trussel. The Alp will not return here. I'm afraid to say we have wasted our time.'

I barely registered what he said. My heart was hammering in my chest and I felt sick, the face of the beast lingering in my memory, pushing all other thoughts aside. When I did not reply, Mr Gout turned to me, then placed a hand gently on my shoulder.

'Are you alright, Miss Trussel?' he asked softly. 'I'm sorry, I forget what a shock such an experience can be to someone unused to my line of work.'

'I'm...I'm okay,' I managed, not meeting his eye.

'Come,' he said, smiling down at me. 'Let us regroup at your charming bakery. I feel a cup of tea and a custard tart coming on.'

PART THREE

We spoke little on our return journey, both lost in thoughts of our own, and arrived back at the bakery to find my mother behind the counter. I'd hoped to avoid her. We had yet to discuss the results of my trip to the job fair the previous day, and I was not looking forward to explaining my failure.

The minute she saw me, she beckoned me over, her face stern. I could tell she'd had a stressful morning by the tight line of her mouth and the wisps of grey hair that had escaped from her bun.

'Where have you been?' she demanded, glancing at Mr Gout as he followed me up to the counter. 'You could have told me you'd be out all morning. I've been stuck behind this counter and your father needs help with tomorrow's orders.'

I hung my head. 'Sorry, Mother,' I said, then paused, considering how much I should tell her about the events of the last twenty-four hours. My mother had always been a practical sort of woman. I could imagine her reaction to the story of the Alp only too well. Fortunately, Mr Gout came to my rescue, stepping forward and bowing over-formally.

'I'm most terribly sorry, my dear lady. The fault is entirely mine! Mr Gout, at your service. I detained young Clementine here longer than I should. You see, I have most particular needs and must question each candidate carefully.'

My mother looked at him with sharp eyes. I could see her thoughts play across her face. 'Candidate?'

Mr Gout nodded, smiling at her in his disarming way. 'Indeed. For the position of assistant house-keeper.'

My mother's face lit up. 'I see. Well, you won't find a harder worker than our Clementine. I've made sure of that.'

'I've no doubt that's true,' Mr Gout replied, beaming.

'Would you care to come in for a drop of tea?' my mother asked, her eyes calculating.

'That would be most agreeable. I was just saying to your daughter how I had the craving for a custard tart or two. I don't suppose...?' Mr Gout said, leaving the sentence hanging.

'It would be my absolute pleasure!' my mother said, warming to her role as hostess. 'Please, come through.'

She lifted part of the counter and ushered Mr Gout through. I followed them into the small sitting room where I had sat with Mr Gout the night before.

'How charming!' he said, giving a convincing performance of seeing the room for the first time.

'Why don't you fetch the tea and custard tarts while I speak to Mr Gout here?' my mother said to me, before fixing him with the largest smile I had seen her face produce in years. 'Do sit down, sir.'

I left the room reluctantly, unsure of exactly what Mr Gout was planning. I took the opportunity to check on Granny, whose breathing had become more steady, although she was still unconscious. I returned to the living room some ten minutes later with the tea to find the two of them deep in conversation about – of all things – the little stone bridge that led into the town. Mr Gout was extolling its many virtues as a fine example of its kind, and my mother was emphatically agreeing, nodding along.

'Oh, you are quite right, Mr Gout, quite right. We are, of course, very proud of it in the town.'

I had to stop my mouth from falling open. I had never heard her express an opinion on the bridge one way or another before that night. Indeed, I had never given it much thought myself.

'Ah, refreshments! How fabulous. I'm positively famished!' cried Mr Gout, upon seeing me in the doorway.

'Well then, you simply must stay for lunch later,' my mother said.

'Oh, well, I should hate to impose.'

'Nonsense. I won't take no for an answer!' she insisted, in mock admonishment.

'Then it would be churlish for me to refuse!' Mr Gout replied.

There followed one of the strangest thirty minutes of my young life, during which my mother – a woman not known for her sociability – and our exuberant guest held animated discussions on a range of topics, from the health of the ducks in a nearby millpond, to the rising price of bread flour, via the virtues of a solid education in the classics. I remained mostly silent throughout, sipping my tea and nibbling my tart, wondering just how much more peculiar my week could get.

Eventually, Mr Gout gave a great sigh of satisfaction and said, 'Well, this has been most pleasant, Mrs Trussel, most pleasant indeed. But I really must interview young Clementine here. Just a formality, I'm sure, but in the interest of fairness…'

'But of course, sir!' my mother said, smiling brightly. 'I shall go and see about lunch. You be sure to answer Mr Gout's questions honestly and fully now, Clementine.'

'Of course, Mother,' I replied as she bustled out of the room.

Alone once again, I looked to Mr Gout for some clue to his plan. His smile had disappeared as soon as my mother left the room. I felt tired, dispirited and more than a little anxious about the fate of Granny.

'What do we do now?' I asked.

Mr Gout sighed. 'I'm afraid there is little to do now but wait for the creature to make its next appearance.'

'You mean wait for it to attack Granny again!'

He nodded solemnly. 'Yes. Now it has fled its lair, there is really no other way of tracking it down. But based on what you've told me, its pattern seems clear. It will return to feed off your grandmother and

I believe it will do so tonight.'

'But...but we can't let it! You said yourself she wouldn't survive another attack.'

'Fear not, my dear girl: I will allow no harm to befall your grandmother, or indeed any other member of your family,' Mr Gout assured me.

My expression must have betrayed my thoughts as he gave an irritated little harrumph and said, 'I know this morning's unfortunate events may not have instilled in you much confidence in my abilities, but I assure you, I really am rather good at this sort of thing.'

'But that's just it, Mr Gout. I'm not sure I understand exactly what sort of thing this is. Or what you plan to do about it.'

He nodded, giving me a small smile. 'Perhaps it is time I explained further. You have seen the beast in its true form now, after all, so you should have no problem in accepting the details of the matter.'

'I'm ready!' I said.

Mr Gout then fixed his blue eyes on me most inquiringly. 'How do you feel about magic?'

I thought for a moment. 'Something tells me you're not talking about top hats and white rabbits.'

He made a face. 'Nonsense and trickery!'

'Then I think that I know nothing about magic at all, and will reserve my judgement until I do,' I continued.

Mr Gout nodded, satisfied. 'Good answer. Although magic is not inherently evil, those who wield it are not always pure of intention. It is not something to be trifled with, as we've seen from our hat-wearing friend. An Alp is not something one spontaneously becomes; it is something that is deliberately made. By someone with a lot of power.'

'So, you're saying that this person – the one who became the Alp that's been attacking Granny – had this done to them? They're a victim too?'

'Quite right.'

'But...why? Why would anyone do that to someone? What's to be gained? Or are you saying that someone set this thing on my Granny deliberately? That she's the target?'

Mr Gout shook his head. 'I think that's unlikely. This kind of magic can be unpredictable. It would be impossible for the spell-caster to know exactly who the Alp would latch onto after it was created. No, I think it far more likely that the spell was cast as a punishment on the unfortunate soul itself. Quite the torment, when you think about it. Doomed to walk the earth, not dead, but not alive either. Drawn by irresistible urges to feed off others to survive.'

I shivered at the thought, glad to be safe inside the walls of our small, snug sitting room. The feeling faded as I remembered our house must have been infiltrated by the Alp many times. This was not something happening out there: it was here, in the very heart of my quiet life.

I swallowed hard and asked, 'So how do we break the spell? You said we can't simply destroy the hat.'

'That's where things get tricky, I'm afraid,' Mr Gout replied. It was odd to see him so serious after hearing him discuss ducks and bridges with my mother so jovially just minutes before. 'To reverse the spell, I must use a particular incantation. It is already known to me, so that part is simple enough, but in order for the spell to be effective, I must use the victim's real name. Which means we must find out who they were.'

My heart sank. 'But how will we ever be able to find that out?'

'We have one important clue: your grandmother.'

'Granny? But I thought you said she wasn't the target?'

'Correct. However, an Alp will most likely feed off someone known to them in their previous life. Therefore, if we are to save them both, we must hope your grandmother has some idea who it might be.'

My eyes went to the ceiling, imagining the frail form of Granny in her small bedroom above. 'She has been unconscious since last night. She isn't in a position to tell us anything.'

Mr Gout inclined his head, looking grave. 'Precisely why I had hoped to capture the Alp this morning. It would have bought us time for your grandmother to recover. But we must not cry over spilt milk, and trust that she will wake before the Alp arrives to feed.'

Lunch became a rather drawn-out affair. Mother rustled up an impressive table of cold meats, cheese and pastries considering the short notice, and Mr Gout was able to satisfy what I was learning to be his prodigious appetite, all the while deftly avoiding my mother's increasingly unsubtle questions about the likelihood and nature of my future employment.

As the afternoon wore on and the winter light began to fade, I could tell she was becoming exasperated. Had it been anyone else, I felt sure she would have shown them the door long ago. However, with my gainful employment hanging in the balance, she obviously felt compelled to continue pandering to the eccentric man who appeared disinclined to leave her home.

My father had appeared briefly, been thoroughly startled by the presence of a man he didn't know sitting at his dining table, then retreated to the safety of the shop counter as soon as politely possible. When my three brothers returned home from school, they stood staring at Mr Gout with their mouths open as though he were a performing monkey. Toby, the youngest, looked likely to poke our guest's bulging stomach with a stick he had acquired on his way home until my mother ushered them away with embarrassment.

'Please forgive my boys. It has been some time since we've had a guest of your...quality in our house.'

Mr Gout had spent the afternoon wearing an almost perpetual beaming smile, and he turned it on my mother then. 'Not at all, my dear Mrs Trussel. A healthy curiosity is a sign of an inquiring mind.'

There then came a long stretch of awkward silence until my mother exclaimed, for what must have been the tenth time, 'Well, isn't this nice!'

'Indeed,' said Mr Gout. Then, as if receiving a silent signal of some kind, he added, 'Perhaps you should check on your poor grandmother, Clementine? Didn't you say she was ill?'

I jumped up and left the room before my bewildered mother could stop me, taking the stairs two at a time and slowing only when I reached the entrance to Granny's room. I opened the door silently, unsure of what I would find inside, but was greeted only by the sight of my sleeping grandmother, illuminated by the last of the pale light from the window, just as I had left her. I crept to the window to check it was still firmly closed. As I did so, Granny let out the tiniest mumble. I rushed to her side, hoping she was waking up at last, but was disappointed to find her eyes still shut.

'Granny? It's Clementine. Can you hear me?'

I waited, but there was no response. I looked around the darkening room, but seeing nothing out of place and there being no further sign of life from Granny, I left. But just before the door clicked closed, I heard the faintest creak, like the groaning of old wood under pressure.

The window frame!

I threw the door back open just in time to see the foul figure of the Alp, in human form and with the derby hat still firmly on its head, drop from the now open window onto the floor of the room. It started at the movement of the door and bared its teeth at me, hissing violently, before rearing up and changing shape, morphing into the form of a giant snake. It towered over me and a scream ripped itself from my throat. I expected I would feel the bite of its pointed teeth rip into me at any second and so was more than a little shocked when instead the snake began to shrink, soon becoming the regular size for such creatures, before slithering under the bed and disappearing. I had barely recovered from my surprise when I heard the faint protestations of my mother from below, followed by the thundering noise of someone running up the stairs, and Mr Gout arrived at my side, breathing hard.

'It is here?'

I nodded dumbly, then managed, 'Under the bed. Snake.'

He glanced at me, checking I was unhurt, before hastening into the room. 'We must not let it leave! Close the door and find something to block the keyhole while I get the window. It can get through even the smallest gap!'

He lurched towards the window, wrenching it closed with a bang that woke me from my stupor. I stepped sharply into the room, pulling the door shut behind me. On the bedside table lay a handkerchief, which I snatched up and stuffed into the keyhole. Then, for good measure, I took a blanket and lay it across the bottom of the door, squeezing it into the crack between the door and the floor. I straightened up and turned, just in time to see my Granny's bed leap a foot off the floor.

'It has changed again,' Mr Gout warned. 'Be ready.

It will not be pleased when it finds there's no escape.'

At that moment, as if in response to his words, the Alp erupted from under the bed, now in the shape of a large, snarling dog. The bed itself catapulted back violently against the wall and my grandmother slid to the floor in a heap. I heard her moan as she hit the ground.

'We need that name, Clementine!' Mr Gout cried. 'You must get it from her whilst I start the incantation!'

All very well, I thought, but there was the small matter of the enraged dog between me and her. Mr Gout had reached inside his jacket and produced a battered leather notebook, which he was now flicking through hastily, muttering to himself.

'Now, did I put it under A for Alp or I for incantation?'

I would have to face the dog alone. My eyes ransacked the room, desperate for something to defend myself with. They alighted on the smooth wooden handle of a brass bedpan that had been hidden under the bed. I grabbed for it desperately as the dog advanced towards me, growling and hackles raised. It leapt, and I swung, bringing the bedpan round in an arc that connected with a crunch in the creature's face. Unfortunately, it was at that moment I realised the bedpan had not been emptied, and I watched helplessly as the contents continued on its sweeping arc, splattering into the unprepared Mr Gout, who gave a cry of revulsion.

'Really, Miss Trussel!' he protested, looking down

at his soiled waistcoat. 'Do be careful!'

'Sorry!'

'Oh, now look at that, the words have all run!'

'I said I was sorry!' I repeated, bringing the offending instrument down on the dog's head for a second time. It whimpered and suddenly became a pig, which squealed at me furiously as Mr Gout began to chant in words that I did not understand.

'Stop! Don't hurt him!'

The cry came from across the room, and I turned to see that Granny was awake and pulling her weak body to a sitting position beside the upset bed. There came a pounding on the bedroom door and I heard the muffled sound of my mother from the other side.

'What is going on in there, Clementine? Open this door at once! Really, Mr Gout, this is completely unacceptable!'

'Just a moment, my good woman!' Mr Gout called sweetly before returning to his strange chant.

The words seemed to enrage the Alp, and it began to change shape again, becoming a roiling green-black mass as it shifted from pig to dog to snake to humanoid.

'Granny!' I cried desperately. 'His name, we need his name!'

My grandmother shook her head feebly, tears trickling down her pale face. 'No...no...don't hurt him, please!'

'We won't,' I promised. 'We just want to set him free. Please, Granny, his name!'

But my grandmother just shook her head, weeping.

The Alp had now settled into its human form and at the sound of Granny's sobs, it gave the most heart-wrenching howl I have ever heard. I rushed to the old woman's side, taking her hands in mine and looking deep into her tear-stained face.

'Trust me!'

She looked into my eyes for what felt like the longest time, and in hers I saw a pain I had never noticed before. But eventually, she whispered, 'Stephen. It's Stephen.'

Mr Gout must have heard because the volume of his chanting increased and he stepped towards the Alp purposefully. As his words reached their crescendo, he lunged towards the beast and whipped the derby hat from its head at the exact moment he cried, 'Stephen!'

The effect was instantaneous. Before us, where the Alp had been, now stood a man. Or rather, the shadow of a man, for his form was transparent, and he glowed with a soft blue light. He looked to be in his early twenties, strongly built, with a shock of wavy hair and a dimple in the middle of his chin.

'Stephen?' Granny gasped. 'Is it really you?'

The apparition smiled down at her with a look of pure devotion and joy that quite took my breath away. Then, with a sigh like the sound of the waves on a shingle beach, he faded, then disappeared altogether.

'It is over,' said Mr Gout. 'He is at peace.'

At that exact moment my mother finally gained entry to the room, bursting in on us with the sound of splintering wood and an expression of outrage on her face.

'What is going on in here?'

'Ah, Mrs Trussel!' Mr Gout cried, as if welcoming an old friend. 'Your timing is impeccable. We have just, this very moment, ousted a stray dog from your poor mother's room. I'm afraid to say she is quite shaken and may require your gentle touch.'

My mother's eyebrows rose up her face in surprise. 'Dog? I see no dog?'

'We got it out the window. Don't bother looking; it landed on its feet and trotted away. They always land on their feet, dogs,' he replied breezily, making for the door himself.

'I thought that was cats?' said my mother, astonished.

'Really? Oh, well, perhaps it was a cat then. Vicious things. Anyway, I really must be off, lots to do. It's been delightful. I'll let myself out. Ta ta!'

With that, he disappeared down the stairs and we heard the side door open and close as he exited the house. There was an awkward silence for a moment, then my Granny said, 'Who was that peculiar man?'

I learnt the full story two days later. I was sitting once more by my Granny's bedside. The room had been returned to its former state and indeed my grandmother, too, was already looking much healthier.

'Stephen was my first love,' she said with a wistful smile. 'God, it seems a lifetime ago. We were to be married, but he disappeared before the big day. Then one night he returned to me, only he wasn't quite himself anymore. I never did find out what happened, but being with me seemed to soothe him. He wasn't the monster he became, not at the beginning. But the years went by, I met your grandfather, started a family…all the while Stephen still came to me, becoming a little less himself with each visit. Before I knew it, I was an old woman and Stephen – well, I began to wonder if there was anything left of the man I had once known. Despite that, I could not turn him away, for a part of me always loved him. Oh, Clementine, I wish you could have met him as he was! I never met a kinder, more gentle man. I hope he can rest now.'

As for Mr Gout, I had seen no more of him. My mother, clearly unsure how she felt about the whole affair, had elected to say nothing more about it, except to ask on the third night after the Alp's final appearance whether I'd had any news about the job. I told her unfortunately I had not, and her mouth made a little moue of displeasure.

'You know, you needn't worry about Granny. She seems to be recovering nicely,' she said, and I supposed she was right. The thing keeping me in Fairsop was no longer an issue, so perhaps I should find a job. But where? The last few days had effected a change in me like the lifting of a curtain, and the idea of going to some isolated country home and sweeping floors for the next forty years held little appeal. That was why, as I opened the shop the next morning, my heart leapt at the sight of a familiar tweed-clad figure peering in through the window. With a smile on my face, I rushed to unlock the door and let him in.

'My dear Miss Trussel, how delightful to see you!' he cried as he came bouncing into the bakery.

'And you, Mr Gout,' I said, then added, my smile slipping, 'I feared you had left for good.'

He gave a guilty grimace. 'Forgive me, my dear girl. You see, I saw something in the Alp's Tarnkappe that gave me cause for concern. It required looking into.'

I noticed that he was still carrying the black derby hat.

'What did you see?' I asked, immediately curious.

He raised the hat for me to observe and pointed to the bright green feather that was still sticking jauntily out of the band. Up close, I could see a small symbol painted on it in purple ink.

'Is that a lily?' I asked, squinting.

'Yes. And a bad sign.'

'How so?'

'I feel I have come across this mark before. Only I seem to have completely forgotten where. I believe it belongs to a powerful magical practitioner.'

I thought for a moment. 'So you're saying this creature cast the spell that turned Stephen into an Alp? But that happened decades ago. It doesn't mean they're still active today.'

'Unfortunately, that is not necessarily the case. There are magical beings out there for who time is little more than a slightly inconvenient construct; one that they choose to ignore.'

'Oh,' I said.

'I just wish I could remember what I know.' He scratched the spot between his eyes with a portly finger. 'Only trouble is, I have forgotten it, so I don't know what it is I can't remember.'

There followed a few moments of silence. Mr Gout appeared lost in thought and only returned his attention to the here and now when I asked, 'Was there something in particular you wanted, Mr Gout?'

He fixed his blue eyes on mine. 'Ah, well. I believe there was mention of a job.'

'Yes?' I said eagerly.

But his gaze drifted from mine again as he looked at something on the counter behind me. 'I say, are those doughnuts custard or jam?'

THE END

Trussel and Gout will return in:
'Something in the Woodshed'

ACKNOWLEDGEMENT

It has been a long journey getting Mr Gout and his friends out into the world. It could not have been achieved with out the incredible help of a group of equally incredible human beings.

Firstly to my wife Hayley. Your unending support of this crazy author dream of mine means the world to me. You are my muse.

My thanks to Nicola, Sarah, Hanna and Helen. Your early input on Mr Gout has helped shape his world into what it has become.

A huge thanks to Nick Hodgeson of Root-and-branch editing, whose expert advise polished this manuscript until it shone. Any remaining mistakes are mine alone.

The #writingcommunity on instagram have been an unending source of wisdom and support. The #booktok community on Tiktok have also been amazing in their enthusiasm for the release of this story. You are legion, and far too many to mention here. You know who you are.

My especial thanks to my beta readers. Your love and support of theses stories spurred me on, when I might otherwise have given up.

ABOUT THE AUTHOR

M.a.knights

Hello. I'm M.A.Knights, an English writer living in the glorious countryside of wild west Wales. Here the rugged cliffs, rolling hills and ever-changing sea inspire the worlds of my creation. After achieving a BSc in Countryside Conservation and an MSc in Geographic Information and Climate Change, I realised I am, in fact, not a scientist at all. It's the what-do-you-call-it? ... memory! Not what it used to be, don't you know? And what with all those numbers and things ... dreadful! Simply dreadful. So I've left the data crunching to those cleverer than I and instead have returned to the fantastical imaginings of my youth. I hope one day to lose myself in a world of my own creation.

Inspired by writers like Terry Pratchett, P.G.Wodehouse, Tom Holt and Jasper Fforde, I revel in the creation of fantastical worlds full of improbable beasts and eccentric, larger than life characters.

Printed in Great Britain
by Amazon